John Todhunter

Helena in Troas

John Todhunter

Helena in Troas

ISBN/EAN: 9783744729017

Printed in Europe, USA, Canada, Australia, Japan

Cover: Foto ©Andreas Hilbeck / pixelio.de

More available books at **www.hansebooks.com**

HELENA IN TROAS

BY

JOHN TODHUNTER

AUTHOR OF

"LAURELLA, AND OTHER POEMS," "ALCESTIS," "A STUDY OF SHELLEY,"
"THE TRUE TRAGEDY OF RIENZI." "FOREST SONGS," ETC.

" Was this the face that launched a thousand ships,
And burnt the topless towers of Ilium ?
Sweet Helen, make me immortal with a kiss ! "

LONDON

KEGAN PAUL, TRENCH & CO., 1, PATERNOSTER SQUARE

1886

TO

LOUIS C. PURSER,

FELLOW OF TRINITY COLLEGE, DUBLIN,

IN GRATITUDE FOR MUCH HELP CORDIALLY GIVEN,

I DEDICATE THIS POEM.

B

DRAMATIS PERSONÆ.

— ——

PRIAM.

PARIS.

HECUBA.

HELENA.

ŒNONE.

Chorus of Trojan Women.

———

Time occupied in the action : from sunrise to sunset.

HELENA IN TROAS.

SCENE.—*Before the Palace of Priam.*

CHORUS.

Strophe.

Wail, Ilion, wail for the day of thy desolation !

Wail with thy breezy towers ! To thy shuddering
    gates we throng,

Desperate drops of life to the heart of a dying nation.

Menacing woe, singing a terrible song !

Woe ! woe ! For, as wolves in winter, squadrons of
    fears

Gather by night to devour us, out of the air,

Fears, fierce-eyed fears ; nor fly they at dawn, but
    glare

Round us, after us, everywhere :

In the cheek-chilled brine of our tears
Scenting the curdled blood of biers.
O house, desolate house,
Palace of Priam, thy dolorous gates
Open to us, that we may carouse
With the ghosts of thy dead, with the hovering fates
Of thy dwindled living, whom Death allows
A pale respite while he waits !
O quiver emptied, thy shafts in vain
Wasted, squandered upon the plain !
Thy golden chambers are silent cells
Where richly Desolation dwells :
And wildly we, her mænads, come
Wailing to thy gates, each lip
Wan for dread of the spoiler's ship,
The ravisher's bed, the tyrant's loom
Of loveless labour, and servile whip.

Epode.

Surge, surge of the sea,
Wilt thou sweep us like weeds away
Weak spoil of yon trampled strand,
Where Paris, while feet were free
And the dreamer might dreaming stray,

Toward the sunset for Helen's sake
Sighing, the lonely sand
Paced in his manhood's pride ;
Where out of the siren foam
Soft, foam-born murmurs came
Soft to his ear, as in Ida spake
The Foam-born once and his heart replied,
Remurmuring Helen's name :
And he recked not, though scornèd Pallas, in scorn,
Turned from us, wroth for his choosing, and dread
Fell from her ægis, and gloom o'er thee,
When he sailed with the wind of an evil morn,
Impious, over thee, surge of the sea,
To the spoil of a Spartan bed !

Y

HELENA, CHORUS.

CHORUS.

Look where, reborn in beauty, fresh as dawn
New-risen from grey Tithonus' bed, she comes,
This golden Ate by the Olympian scorn
Flung back on Paris' hand, to plague the world
With ruin's share driven red o'er homes of men !

HELENA.

Mother of winds, whom in the dawn of things
To holiest Hyperion Thea bore,
Bringer of day to mortals, Eos, lo,
Touched by thy dewy fingers—such a wind
Of fate upon my soul as o'er strange seas
Swept me from the Spartan couch I knew no more,
Leaving a more luxurious now I come,
With heart on fire, the homeless Helena,
A name of glory and shame !   For me the gods
Have given a twofold fortune, and a doom
Beyond all doom of women good and ill.

CHORUS.

Curst be thy beauty for the woes of Troy !

HELENA.

Ye hold, with grief-wrung mind, a scale unjust,
Blaming the cup made splendid by the gods
To be the prize of fame's fierce chariot-race
For perils of the course.   Why curse ye me ?

CHORUS.

We curse the cup of our calamities,

The tarnished beaker, full of maddening wine,
Lipped by a hundred heroes, drained by none,
Cursing thy beauty for the woes of Troy.

HELENA.

Hung be the woes of Troy around my neck
For dreadful amulets ! Here unabashed
I stand, that Helena whose beauty's might
Sinewed the fiery valour of her time,
And made on Clio's lips the tale of Troy
A thunderous murmur of immortal names.
Mine are the deeds of heroes done for me,
Hector and great Achilles ; and my face,
Gilding with glory the red woof of war,
Shall shine for ever in the hearts of men.
O, thus I shed my beauty on the winds,
To fly, a mailèd Pallas, through the world,
And wake such battle as delights the gods !

CHORUS.

Madness hath fallen upon thee from the gods !

HELENA.

Or haply Death draws near me, like a bard,

Chanting to his deep lyre oracular things.

CHORUS.

But here comes one to smite thy pride with speech,
The mournful mother of sons dead by thee.

Y.

HECUBA, HELENA, CHORUS.

HECUBA

Do I behold the fatal fire of Troy?

HELENA.

We are what we are, mother : am I that fire?

HECUBA.

Ay, fire thou art, kindling the brand I bore.

HELENA.

The brands I kindle shine immortal stars.

HECUBA.

I speak of him, the firebrand of my dream.

HELENA.

Paris : thy pride, bearing me from his bark?

HECUBA.

Ay, him thy beauty snared to ruin Troy.

HELENA.

Proud wast thou once to kiss me for his sake.

HECUBA.

For deadliest fruits the gods gild to the eye.

HELENA.

Poor fruit, of gods and plucker bear the guilt !

HECUBA.

Do wantons guileless mesh the souls of men ?

HELENA.

Sail women o'er the seas to ravish men ?

HECUBA.

Wantons beguile not women, nor thou me.

HELENA.

Women should pity women—I do thee.

HECUBA.

O pitiless mischief ! Thee no woman bore,

Wooed by the billing of the amorous swan ;
Yea, Leda bore thee not, but Nemesis,
To be the doom of Troy and Priam's house.

HELENA.

Yet, being a woman, I can pity thee.

HECUBA.

Thou art no woman ; for thou hast no heart
To warm the splendid marble of that breast,
No homestead, nor no children ; knowest no love ;
Thou art a thing kindless, and subtly framed
Of elemental cruelty, like the gods
Who have gendered thee and evil : and both I know.

HELENA.

I have no heart to cast forth new-born babes ;
If this be woman's wont, then am I none.

HECUBA.

O Hector, thou art gone, thy valorous arm
A pinch of feeble dust ; yea Troy is down,
And I already captive to the spear
Of some red-handed murderer of my joy :

I must feed on gall, derision with my tears
Drink ; for this Fury mocks me ! To be chaste,
Mother of men, an honourer of the gods,
Is to be wretched, scorned, plagued by the gods ;
Who cherish us for their gain, slay for their sport,
Taming the strong with fraud, the weak with fear ;
Who are swift as vultures to the sobbing throat
Of the hurt quarry, slayers of things slain.

CHORUS.

Many and bitter plagues the gods on men
Loose ; the just eye alone perceives them just.

HECUBA.

What ægis guards the oppressed ? What golden bow
Makes void the oppressor's throne, save, god with
     god
Warring, we pay their feud ? Who shall be just
Of mortals, when the Immortals dare not look
In the holy eyes of Justice ; yet are bold
To laugh behind the flying of her feet
Cast out from high Olympus, in the void
With unbegotten dreams to wander and wait ?

CHORUS.

O Queen ! the mist of tears is but a cloud
Hiding the sun in heaven, and impious words,
The abortions of our pride, Titans too weak
To scale the mount where Truth looks every way.

HECUBA.

Talk to the sun-sick Naiad where she pines
Among her sere-tongued sedges, shrunk from June's
Hot lips upon her parched and dwindled stream,
Whose eyes are filled with fire, whose throat with dust,
Of her spent waters, ere to me of tears.
I am dry as ashes, who have brought forth fire
To quench the fire of my hearth, the fire of my life,
A son to slay my sons.   Arraign the pard
That hears with yearning dugs her cubs, far off,
Cry in the hunter's gripe—the restless pard,
Gaunt with fierce hunger of lorn motherhood,
Lashing her tail and roaring—for her moan ;
Not me for my wild words.   I have no words :
My words are wingless woes, that should fly up
Shrill-tongued and shrieking, and like ominous birds
Appal the ear and pale the cheek of Zeus.
But I am weaker than the pinèd leaf

Before the scorns of winter, than the dust
Of the forgotten dead whose broken urn
The sea-wind wantons in.   Lo ! here I sit
Dust in the dust ; for I am Hecuba,
And this is Troy, and I and Troy sink down,
One undistinguishable heap of dust.

CHORUS.

The gods avert the omen of thy words !

HECUBA.

Where are my sons, whose mouths I filled with milk
To be my flower of life, my seed in death ?
With burnt-up harvests, with soon-blighted buds
Vanished in waste.   My emptied arms are cold ;
And I, the woe-worn Niobe of Troy,
Chilled by the glare of Hades' gorgon eyes,
Perish, yet die not.   O, that this heart would burst,
Which still, more tough than the thick-folded hide
Of Hector's shield to fend the shaft of death
From vigorous worth, keeps worthless eld alive !

HELENA.

Mother, wha mother of mortals brings not forth

In shuddering awe each tender shuddering life
To be the quarry of Death, and through the wastes
And glens and tangled thickets of this world
To flee before his hunting?   Late or soon,
The arrow, plumed from his purpureal wing
And dipt in Lethe, finds us, and we sleep.
But cowards, coveting life, he makes his slaves—
Pale shadows in his shadow, their sick day
One pitiful dying ; but the brave he loves,
Who, looking in his eyes, grow like the gods,
And make their hours eternal as their deeds.
And heroes thou hast borne beloved of Death,
So crowned of Life : for what more fits a man
Than a rash life and happy, keen with bliss
And anguish of achievement ; roaring seas
O'ersailed, fair women won, strong sons begot,
The blood and sweat of battle ; then to die,
Where men with gods mingled in glorious strife
Most terribly contend?   O, thus to die,
Heroes by heroes' hands splendidly slain,
Ere she, the mumbling hag with fingers chill,
Old Age, have clutched the heartstrings, is to take
From Death's renowning hand the supreme cup
Of war's red bacchanal ; and these, thy sons,

Are happy in their deaths as in their lives !

HECUBA.

Comfort the starving with thy beauty's bread ;
Soothe festering wounds with kisses ; thrill the ear
Of the cold dead with praise ! then will I laugh
To hear thee strive to cheat the hungry heart
Of sorrow with vain words.   Death, Death has stalked
Too long about my fold, choosing my lambs
For delicate morsels, till the flaring face
Of glory looks as ghastly as thine own :
Yea, thou art glory, and thy beauty's gleam
The luring balefire on a marsh of blood
Whose pools run red with murder of my sons.

HELENA.

Mated with Life thou hast brought forth mortal sons ;
But they grow gods, reborn of me and Death.

HECUBA.

Begone from me, thou plague ! Begone from Troy !
Thy face is grown a sickness in my womb,
I bring forth children dead ! I am smitten through
By thee, a jealous arrow shot from heaven,
A clinging Nemesis, whose vulture wings,

Swift to pursue, soaked in our clogging gore
Forget their swiftness !   Yet have mercy now ;
Spare us at last ; fly, with our guardian gods,
Wise to renounce the fanes of toppling Troy—
Wise as the storks that flap the clanging wing
About our battlements, gathering for flight,
Legioned to steer to countries of the sun !
Lo ! thus I clasp thy knees, pray thee begone
Unto thy kindred and thy husband's house :
Leave us our ruin unruined ; let us weep
The wretched remnant of our days in peace !

HELENA.

Bitter as the salt javelins of the surf.
Launched on a freezing wind, would bite thy words,
Daughter of Kisseus, in a guilty ear ;
But far from mine, who have wronged thee not at all,
They hiss and sing, like random casts of rage.
Is Troy my prize, or I the prize of Troy,
Whose acclamations filled the venturing sail
Of stubborn Paris ; whose possession's pride
Spurred Hector to his slaying ?   But now all
Is changed in Troy, as, when the sun goes down,
Gloom spreads her wings, and melancholy winds

Blow from the sepulchres of mighty kings ;
And hope renews not, though the dreadful crest
Of fierce Achilles, by thy bolt and mine,
Be sunk as low as Hector's, whom he slew :
Now therefore, if the keen desire of war
Have lost its edge, take me and send me back
Unto the angry chiefs, to save or slay
As the stern Fates decree.   But lo! where comes
The lorn grey majesty of Priam's head,
Bent from the kissing of those murderous hands.

PRIAM, HECUBA, HELENA, CHORUS.

PRIAM.

I hear the voice of women in my gates,
And clamours of the Queen.   With what new face
Looks the old woe upon my falling house ?

HELENA.

Hail, hoary seed of Zeus, and reverend sire !

PRIAM.

And hail to thee, daughter!   But what dear name
Spoken to-day is grown a theme of tears?

HECUBA.

The new day's new fear, as yet, is all the news.

C

PRIAM.

But in mine ear sounded a voice of wail?

HECUBA.

There smiles the ancient woe, that day by day
Renews, to our new harm, her fatal face.

HELENA.

My feet shall heal the offending of my face.

PRIAM, HECUBA, CHORUS.

PRIAM.

Woe to the town whose war-worn streets are loud
With women's wrangling!   There is barking spite
Unleashed, and loosed the furies of the tongue.
Peace ! for what help is there in clamorous words ?

CHORUS.

When deeds are dead, words are the natural seed
To raise up new : and we have need of words.

PRIAM.

Ye sow the air's barren desert with your tongues,
And reap confusion and revolt of friends.

So, gazing oft from Ilion, have I seen
Above the surge, blackening beneath the wings
Of rushing tempest, scream the land-blown gulls,
Weak in the gusty gloom.   And thou, alas !
What hop'st thou from the windy strife of words ?

HECUBA.

I have no hope ; for hope and thou apart
Cower in the sundered poles.   When sapless age
Has withered up the arm of martial might,
And the shield's strength but hangs about the neck
A weary burthen, and the dreadful spear
Turns to a staff to keep the tottering feet,
Grey hairs should whisper counsel ; but thy head
Is feeble as thy hands to succour Troy.

PRIAM.

What counsel croaks to-day thy raven throat ?

HECUBA.

Send Helen back ere she unpeople Troy ;
Ere treacherous murder, stealing on thy sleep,
With bloody hands uncurtain and profane
Thy hoary head ; ere violent conquest mock
My wasted age with bruise of servile blows.

CHORUS.

Strophe.

Truth is in her ; and hearken thou to her word,
Sire of our State, and venerable King,
Priam, ere some last miserable thing
Swoop on thee like the thunder-bearing bird ;
And Troy be sacked a second time, and thou,
The ransomed, find no ransom : neither gold,
Nor scarf of bright Hesione, who now
Bends o'er the mill with slaves her wrinkled brow,
No ransomed brother for her rescue bold !

PRIAM.

Where shall I hide me from the venomous scourge
Of woman's tongue, of bitterest skill to wound
Again the full of wounds, fret sorest sore
With rancour? Am not I that aged king ;
That beggared majesty ; that red-eyed grief,
All dust and abjectness, with beard defiled,
That startled fell Achilles in his tent
With face so woe begone, with trembling knees
Such pitiful suppliants ; yea with lips so cold
Through anguished kissing of their deadliest bane,

That pity did surprise his furious mood,
As spring soon melting winter, to yield up
The insulted slain, and moved the murderer's eyes
To mingle tears with tears, till his and mine
Whelmed in one sea of sorrow hate with hate ?

HECUBA.

The memory of past sorrows cries aloud
To uproot the root of sorrows yet to come.
Send Helen back, ere she unpeople Troy !

PRIAM.

Hector, our son, is dead ; and now, for staff
Of our much-shaken age, we have but him
To whom, poor babe, cradled with savage beasts,
Thy fear gave cruel nursery : in the glens
Of Ida left to cry for mother's milk
To senseless rocks, hard as his mother's breast !

HECUBA.

An evil fate I bore, for me and thee.

PRIAM.

Our hope revives in him ; before whose bow,
As once the stealthy spoilers of my fold

Bled in the wilds, hath fallen beside our gate
The might of fierce Achilles.   Unto him—
The wind of whose desire raged like a storm
Among the oaks of Ida ; hewing them,
With axes sharper than the autumnal blast
Wields in his ire, to fashion the swift keel
It made to foam beneath the sumptuous load
Of Helen's beauty ; ere, the gift of the sea
Richer than ever amber-bearing wave
Heaped for the treasure-chests of Phrygian kings,
She dawned on shouting Troy—to him, I say,
For he is Helen's lord, prefer thy prayer.

HECUBA.

How meanly shows this letchery of the eye
That fools the greybeard as the smooth-faced boy
Fondly to dote on beauty ; though it prove
But fard upon the cheek of wantonness !
Art thou the king ?   But wherefore, poor old man,
Vex thy decay, whetting the goads of speech
To spur the tardy sides of thy resolve ?
I must be dumb, must garner up my scorn,
Sick to behold grey kingdom sceptreless,
Subject to subjects, and the minished sire

A son to his own son.   Paris is king,
And we in beggar's guise must sue to him !

CHORUS.

Antistrophe.

Youth in his might the leaping surge of the sea,
When all its headstrong brood rush from their caves
To snort in huge and tempest-shouldering waves,
Mates, and outdares in his audacity ;
But a sire's word walks forth in hoary awe,
And sovereign as Poseidon when he rides
O'er monstrous ocean-backs, and tames to draw
His foamy car, slaves to his trident's law,
The flapping tails of all his stubborn tides.

PRIAM.

Hither my beauteous, headstrong billow of youth
Bears Helen on his breast : curb him who can !

PARIS, HELENA, HECUBA, CHORUS.

HELENA.

Farewell ! Thy mother thrusts me forth from Troy.

PARIS.

Nay, by the warrior blood that leaps anew

At sight of thee, in all our valorous veins,
For thy safe-keeping men shall die to-day !

HELENA.

Nay, send me for your safety forth from Troy.

PARIS.

Troy is a stately galley, by the gods
Ribbed and made strong to hold the costliest freight
Clipt in the spacious girdle of the world :
Sink Troy, ere Helen feed the hungry sea !
But blow, blow, ye wild winds ! We defy you yet.

HECUBA.

Our steersman is Despair, and black Defeat
Sits in our sagging sail, and we and Troy
Must feed the hungry sea for Helen's sake :
But see ! I do, what fits me not to do,
Kneel to thee here, the mother to her son,
Beseeching thee by every reverend hair
Silvering thy father's head ; by every tear
I have shed, by every pang I have borne for thee
By every sweet stir of the budding life
In Hector's boy, give not our hoary age
To insult, give not every innocent hope

Yet green about the limbless trunk of Troy
To pitiless slaughter ! O, is a mother's prayer
Weaker to move thee than a wanton's kiss ?

PARIS.

Shame not thy knees, mother ! It is too late
To treat or parley with the vengeful kings
Who, crouched in sullen rage around our walls,
Thirst for our blood, and hunger for our spoil.
All Helen's beauty could not ransom Troy,
Nor ocean's treasure Priam's silvery head ;
But in the last fierce tussle for our lives
Fraud must be tript by fraud ; force tamed by force.
Haply our god-built walls may keep ungorged
These wolves, worn-out with ten years more of siege.

HECUBA.

O'erwise is but a fool ; o'erbold may prove
A pitiful champion. Madness makes thee bold
This woful morn, as madness made thee wise
To drive peace like a beggar from our gates
That day when, heralds from the camp that still
Quaked at Achilles' death, Tydides came
With dark Odysseus ; and a word from thee

Had swept the long threat of the black-prowed ships
From yon polluted beach, heaved Helen's weight
From the sick heart of Troy.   But thou wast swoln
With upstart pride, and soft desire new-born
Of arrogant blood; and here must Helen stay,
To light anew her soon-extinguished torch
Of Spartan nuptial in the flames of Troy.

PARIS.

Would to the gods madness had winged my shaft,
That day of peril, through their herald's vests,
To search the heart of those accursed spies !

HECUBA.

Fraud dreams on fraud, and finds what it suspects.

PARIS.

Simplicity ne'er plumbed Achaian craft.

HECUBA.

Craft genders craft : thine breeds in Grecian minds.

PARIS.

Clasp, then, Odysseus for thy simpler son.

HECUBA.

O snake, that I have nurtured for a son,
Darest thou so sting thy mother! But I see,
As erst thy valour, now thy reverence melts
In the luxurious heat of Helen's arms.

PARIS.

The glow of Helen's arms would make o'erdrowsed
Ambition leap in the heart of mightiest kings.

HECUBA.

Fool! thy ambition dreams but of the doves,
The amorous myrtles, and the trailing skirts
Of Aphrodite, vanquisher of men.

HELENA.

Nay, by the gods, we are not of her train!

PARIS.

Zeus hath two daughters, wonderful, untamed,
Breathers of flame into the souls of men,
Athena, and our Trojan Helena.

HECUBA.

Thine eyes, alas ! blaze with phantastic fire
Dreadful and new.   She, the relentless maid,
Pallas, whom thou hast wronged, in Helen's form
Puffs up thy pride ; as once, with murderous guile,
She stood in semblance of Deiphobus
By valiant Hector, to deliver him up
To base Achilles, who with coward spite
Smote him disarmed.   Thou too through her shalt
     bleed.

PARIS.

My thread spin the dark Fates !   My deeds this day
Speak for me, that the glorious fruit I gave
The Cyprian, not for hers but Helen's sake,
Valour's stern queen ; to hymn whose beauty's praise
Let bards fling wide the sounding gates of speech,
And bid the immortal host of mightiest words
March forth in golden thunders of great song !

HECUBA.

Alas ! thou speak'st, like ruined men run mad,
Vain swelling words ; taking the last mean rags

Of indigence for power's imperial robe.
Bluster no more in Hector's unfilled arms,
But peace, till thou hast done dead Hector's deeds!

PARIS.

I sat in Hector's shade while Hector lived,
And brainless butchery stalked with godlike port
About the plain doing heroic deeds,
Dallying with war; since then I have not slept
Who have made the all-feared Achilles but a ghost.
And now I'll sleep no more till Troy be free,
Or I couch soft in the dusty halls of death.

HECUBA.

Move not the angry spleen that lives in woe
To wish thee suddenly dead, weighing thy worth
With Hector's—O my son, thou art still my son,
And I, thy mother, so distraught and wild
With watching long the slow, sure, strangling close
Of horror's coil, I know not what I say!
And now thy panther spirit, swift and fierce,
Moves mightier thews beneath its velvet fur
Than thy voluptuous youth gave earnest of;
And I must see thee range in dreadful ways

Unmanaged of my hand.   But O, these lunes
Of warrior frenzy fill my soul with fear !
What wilt thou do ?   What can the handful still
Left, the scarred remnant of Achilles' rage,
Do to thrust back the foe so boldly set
In tented watch by our close-leaguered walls ?

PARIS.

Mother, I am belittled by thy spleen,
Being but the son of thy blood, not of thy love
As Hector was : a grief of old, but now
Past mourning.   Yet forbear with ominous tongue
To shake me with the palsy of thy fears,
On whom hangs now the heavy fate of Troy ;
Nor seek with treacherous coils of dark mistrust
To bind my hands, which from old Priam's hands.
Eager to yield, old Priam's sceptre take,
In mine to bud anew.   Here Helen sits,
As firm and native to the fates of Troy
As the Palladium, and as soon shall pass
Beyond our walls to purchase Spartan peace.

HECUBA.

O beauteous serpent, set above thy peers

By dotage of thy sire; too-valued pearl,
Picked from Scamander's ooze to oust the bright
First jewels of his crown! Thou vampire, gorged
Upon thy brothers' blood, wilt thou devour
Thy mother's flesh, thy o'erfond father's head,
For this accursed bride, whose beauty strikes,
Like a pale comet, earth with pestilence!

PARIS.

Good mother, these wild flaws of gusty rage
Shake but my beard, not the meek reverence
A son should bear thee; but now, weary not
Thy tongue with railing at the glorious dawn,
For vain are words to stay the sun in heaven;
But go with me within, and on thy bed
Rest; for the limbs of age have need of rest.

HECUBA.

I am broken, as a tempest-driven wave
Dashed on an iron coast—reel dumbly back,
And have no words! Too strong are evil things!

HELENA, CHORUS.

HELENA.

Now Paris is become the king of Troy,

Mastering this woman's tongue, and I the queen.

CHORUS.

Strange things and ominous have I heard to-day,
And weep not nor rejoice, till flying Time
Ripen the harvest of this furrowed seed.

HELENA.

Thou swift majestic orb, orb of the sun,
Whose rising none can hasten, none delay,
Before whose eager face flee the pale stars
And melancholy clouds, and the wan moon
Withers in heaven !   O terrible spirit of day,
Lord of all winds that heal men or destroy,
Of light and of the lightning ; bringer of cool
Dew from the wandering wells of the great deep
To nourish the tender buds ; pourer of hail
And floods of thunderous rain on harvest fields ;
Fosterer with warmth, parcher with furious heat,
Hear me, for I am thine !   The breast of May
Swells not with ravishment, when o'er the earth
Walks the bright omnipresence of thy love,
More eagerly than mine—for what wild death ?
What kiss deific of divine despair ?

PARIS, HELENA, CHORUS.

PARIS.

Hail! for thy face, O rarest birth of time,
Claims with its glory now the Olympian throne
Kept void for thee in heaven! What shall I do?
What iron deeds that worship may command,
And desperate valour dare to pleasure thee?

HELENA.

The mother of great Theseus was my slave,
Theseus, the touch of whose heroic hand,
Laid like a conqueror's on my virgin breast,
Made in my startled heart the ambitious blood
Leap with strange yearnings. I would have such
        deeds
Done, as would make that Theseus pale in fame,
Achilles but the terror of a dream.

PARIS.

Bid me drag Cerberus to the gates of day!

HELENA.

Vain task! Still me this hunger here! Alas!

D

My pining soul is gnawed by a wolfish want ;
Yet what I want I know not.   I would read
The sibylline secret of the murky eyes
Of lone Persephone, by Orpheus once
Half-charmed, half-ravished from her—half-surprised
Swimming to light upon her passion's tears,
In trancèd hell, when her Lethean blood,
Curdled by Hades' kiss, thrilled to his lyre
And to the dolorous pleading of his voice.

PARIS.

Yet—for thine eyes are, like a sibyl's, grown
Sublime interpreters of starry things—
O, send me forth with favourable words !

HELENA.

Take once again thy name of venturous youth,
Be Alexander, succourer of men,
And armed in that go forth to succour Troy !

PARIS.

Thus, in the radiant morning of thy day,
Wherein I bathe, shall I, at perilous hour
Late come of age, my ardent youth renew.

HELENA.

Haste ; for Death comes with swifter feet than Life,
And hard time's shifting soil to plant with deeds.

PARIS.

O Helen ! by the splendours of that face
Grey Time durst ne'er impeach, and by the wings
Of love that marry me to thy height, I know
That Death, come when he will, shall find our boughs
Decked with the buds of May.   And now, to arms !
For armed by thee I speed to succour Troy.

HELENA.

Speed ; for a piteous flock in desolate fold
Bleeds for thy shepherding.   But with what arms
Of force or craft will thou destroy these foes ?

PARIS.

Craft, which aims well the furious strokes of force.

HELENA.

But how contriving wilt thou smite the strong ?

PARIS.

Heavily falls strength falling into the pit.

HELENA.

What pit shall swallow up the guile of Greece?

PARIS.

My brain mines faster than the sleek-skinned mole.

HELENA.

Who snares Odysseus with the craft of gods?

PARIS.

His heart's a mark fair as Achilles' heel.

HELENA.

Upon this warier game how creep'st thou close?

PARIS.

The hunter's craft flies on the veering winds,
Answering each moment's call, and hour by hour
I'll breed new phantasies, changeful as clouds
By Hermes spun, to cheat the hundred eyes
Of sleepless Argus; playing gloriously
For glorious stakes, life, Troy, and Helena.

HELENA.

With arms, not brains, the game is played at last.

PARIS.

I, the quick brain, move many a vigorous arm,
Wield, like my sinewed frame, my nimble host
Picked from the best of **Troy**; ruling like Zeus
This many-headed Titan, limbed with men
And trained to skirmish with the dexterous play
Of Polydeuces' fists—no scrambling rout
Of Hector's squandered thousands, random led.

HELENA.

Bring it to action's proof, test means with deeds.

PARIS.

To-day we'll open our ne'er-opening gates,
And thou shalt watch me, with my archer band
Horsed on the progeny of the winds—our steeds
Of the fleet stock that once upon the mares
Of wealthiest Erichthonius Boreas got—
Harass the foe; shaming the angry scud
Of tempest-clouds, that shoot their arrowy plague
Of stinging sleet and terribly vanish.   I,

Stern as Apollo from the whirlwind's blast
Aiming at Niobe's sons, my quiver stored
With heroes' deaths, will waste no shaft : but once
If my shrill bowstring cry, one enemy's heart
Shall feel the messenger of Troy's revenge.

HELENA.

Go, with the augury of fortunate words,
And victor come : let me not fall again
Into the bloody, cold, and treacherous hands
Of the accursèd house of Tantalus !

PARIS.

Thy tyrant shall not live, with furious blade
To threat the beauteous breast of Helena.

HELENA.

Nay, though my beauty's sorcery should grow weak
To turn the threatening points of angry swords,
I should not die.   In Menelaus' mind
There is no manhood for that stern revenge.
He'd have me meanly live, not proudly die.

PARIS.

Live then, to reign with me in rescued Troy !
But come, thy hand shall arm me for the fight,

Thine eyes shed victory on me from the wall.

CHORUS.

Strophe.

O thou divine one, who, filled with the Thunderer,
Lightnings immortal divinely conceiving,
Long o'er the world with thy burden of sorrow
Didst wearily wander !
Leto, thee we invoke, whose life
Long through her, of thy mighty lover
The ox-eyed, jealous consort, through Hera,
Panted, a shelterless hunted fear !
But over the sleep of the eyeless ocean,
A startled, timorous quail thou fleddest
To Delos, harbouring Delos ;
For firm it stood, earth-shaking Poseidon
For thee, the wanderer, the wanderer staying
With weight of his pitying trident ;
And there in the halcyon sleep of the ocean,
From the eyes of her envy, the beak of her malice,
Deep-hidden, baffling the furious Python,
Thou didst welcome the sacred pangs ;
For there dwelt peace and the shadowing olive,
There, clasping safely the roots of succour,

Didst thou, on earth, for the thrones of heaven
Bring forth gods, and a race of gods!

Antistrophe.

Thee too, O radiant archer invincible,
Glad from the sorrowful breast of thy mother
Born, as a song from the lips of a singer,
Bright flower of her passion!
Phœbus, thee we exalt, whose bow
Sternly bent, with avenging arrows
To plague that plague, prevailed, and the Python
Smote, and delivered the weak from fear!
And Cynthia by thee, thy buskined sister,
Ye ranged the world on the winds of heaven,
Olympians, claiming Olympus;
Ye poured divinely scorn on the scorner,
And terribly, your mother's avengers,
The storm of your pitiless shooting;
And now to thy hands, O Pythian Apollo
Of the lyre and the bow, has the Thunderer given
To wield the might of the dreadful ægis,
Tame with terror the march of pride;
And thou alone of the throned Immortals
Canst face the frown of the eager Virgin,

The grey-eyed, terrible ægis-bearer,
Thou alone of the sons of Zeus !

Epode.

And now, O victress o'er many foes,
Pity our fear !
For jealous Hera hath sent against us,
Out of the bitter sea, a plague ;
And up from the threatening deep no god
Lifts in pity his hoary head,
Over the weltering surge no Delos
Soothes the aching of weary eyes.
And thou whose beauty rejoices heaven
And comforts earth ! with what voice, what vows,
By which of thy sacred names appealing,
Shall we entreat thee to be our succour ?
Swift, for we love thee, rise and deliver us,
Delian !   Pythian !
Come with help in thy golden bow,
Pæan !   Thymbræan !

PARIS, CHORUS.

PARIS.

Ah, me ! I burn !

CHORUS.

Where dost thou ail?   What fate hath fallen on thee?

PARIS.

I burn! I burn!

CHORUS.

Thou writhest truly; yet I see no fire.

PARIS.

No, none that green Ida with all her streams
Could cool, or old Scamander's iciest waves
Rushing in spring; no nor the emptied urns
Of all the seas that hear Poseidon's voice
Quench; the vast ocean were a drop of dew
Poured in this Phlegethon!   O Heracles,
This is thy stroke—twice hast thou ruined Troy!
Ah, me! I burn!

HELENA, PARIS, CHORUS.

HELENA.

What strange and ghastly outcry rends mine ear?

PARIS.

Ah ! Helen, Helen !

HELENA.

What dreadful tale glares dumbly from thine eyes ?

PARIS.

The doom of Troy—lost, lost for Helen's sake !

HELENA.

Of Troy I ask not, but of thee what news ?

PARIS.

My blood is seething fire—I burn ! I burn !

HELENA.

What fire or whence ?   Kindled of men or gods ?

PARIS.

A dead man, and a live man, and the gods.

HELENA.

Whence may a dead man's hand find power to wound?

PARIS.

Shafts from a dead man's bow fly swift and far.

HELENA.

But by whose hand art thou, the striker, struck?

PARIS.

By Heracles I die, like Heracles.

HELENA.

But he by Deianeira's poisoned robe.

PARIS.

One death we die, scorched by the Hydra's blood.

HELENA.

Alas! whence falls this fiery venom now?

PARIS.

The bow of Heracles is come to Troy.

HELENA.

A pledge of doom! But borne within whose hand?

PARIS.

Of all thy suitors grimmest looks this groom.

HELENA.

At last limps Philoctetes to the field?

PARIS.

Ay, and hath shot one shaft, and Troy is down.

HELENA.

Where slept thine archery that one shaft he shot?

PARIS.

The crafty plot, the fated comes to pass.

HELENA.

By Zeus! thou shalt not die, if there be found
Theriac beneath the sun to give thee life.
Send heralds forth, and let Machaon come
With Podalirius from the Achaian host,
And send me to my Spartan for this grace.

PARIS.

Rather my sword should end me, having first

Sent thee to shine beside thy brother stars !
But no, no sword of mine with hideous wound
Could mar the splendid wonder of thy breast :
And I am dying, dying while I gaze !

HELENA.

Full evil is thy fate and mine ; for now
Thou diest, when thy soul had grown so great
To champion me.   Thou shalt not die ! though now
Death find thee not unpraised of Helena,
Nor honoured less than Hector with her tears.
But come, for thou art faint, and, where the fresh
Breeze of the sea kisses this marble cool,
Rest, and let surgery seek to bring thee ease.

PARIS.

Bring me no ease awhile, for ease is death ;
Nor touch me, lest thou perish in my fire.

HELENA.

Would to the gods thy lips could kiss me dead.
For I am homesick for some world unknown !

PARIS.

Nay, I but wronged thy beauty with my fear :

There is no fire in me to kindle thee
With this thy torment, as no virtue, alas !
To pluck the flower of thy divine desire.
O mystery of perfection, bared to sight
To mock the searching of the unlidded eye
That aches on thee ! Immaculate womanhood,
Possessed, yet never won ! O river of bliss,
Where, deeper plunged than vexèd Tantalus,
I stand, and gape with my deluded lips
To assuage the thirst that fills me at thy sight !
Cold Cynthia once in love's abandonment
Stooped upon Latmos ; thou and Pallas brook
No moment of surrender. But I rave,
Who am content with longing, nothing blame,
Nothing repent, nothing bewail ; so thou
Draw near, and let me gaze into thine eyes,
And make these pangs voluptuous with thy touch !

HELENA.

What thou canst win from me I freely give,
And more I may not, while the Fates endure,
Who grimly span, with tender threads and stern
The passionate fibres of this mateless heart ;
For some they have shaped to twine a happy home

With gentle tendrils that caress and cling :
Not me, who am as the flower of some fair tree
Cast on the angry seas, upon what coast
Their boisterous contention sets unto
Stranded awhile ; then back into the surge
Whirled in a moment.   Outrage is my praise,
My glory ravishment !   But, enough ; mine ear
Awaits the bitter burthen of thy tongue.

PARIS.

In ruin's flash moments loom vast as years,
Yet brief shall be my tale.   Six times my bow
Had, like the hawking swallow, twittered shrill,
And six times fallen a chief, clutching in vain
With baffled fingers at the vampire thing,
Steeped to the plumes in blood, that drank his life.
Then, as I held my hand in mere disdain,
Looking for worthier quarry, I beheld
Odysseus glittering in Achilles' arms ;
And murmuring : " Hear, Thymbræus, and, though
          I die,
Grant me yon fox's life ! " my seventh shaft
Notched on the string, I strained to find some gate
Wherethrough to speed my messenger of death.

But he points with his spear : a muffled shape,
Couched on the earth, rose gaunt ; and through this
    arm
Shot, with a fiery pang, the bolt of doom,
Hissing like hate—a hydra-headed bane
Plumed from the wings of those Stymphalian birds,
Its venom stung from soaring ; and, still unseen
Through speed, went hissing on. As dropped my
    bow
I saw Odysseus peer at me and smile ;
But Philoctetes, whose cold eye disdained
To follow to its mark his grizzly bolt,
Turned on his heel, and back into his tent
Sullenly stalked ; and left in me this fire.

HELENA.

O, bend thy wit to grapple with this woe
That swoops upon us now ! Is there no help
In Troy : none skilled in sage Apollo's art,
With healing gum, or herb of potent juice,
Or oozèd distillation of sweet balms,
To medicate the wound : no agèd crone,
Or sorceress of Medea's sisterhood—
Who knows, with muttered spell, when at full moon

E

Or new she culls her simples, how to charm
Night-opening flowers to keep unshed their dew
With starry influence dim—whose subtle craft
May work soft witchery in thy burning blood,
Soothed with some cold elixir magical?

PARIS.

One hope there is; but that to think were shame.

HELENA.

Give me the hope, and I'll endure the shame.

PARIS.

A woman holds my life within her hand.

HELENA.

How sounds her name upon the lips of men?

PARIS.

O name, once loved, sleeping in memory's cave
Long years of silence, must I utter thee now!
Forlorn Œnone, fount of passionate tears;
O lonely dweller in the dim, sweet glades
Of Ida, is thine hour of vengeance come!

HELENA

What is she; and what spell casts on thy life ?

PARIS.

The beauteous daughter of a river-god,
Old Kebren's daughter, whose white-ankled feet
Over the sward of Ida gleamed, how oft !
Fleet-tripping through the dew to meet her love,
The shepherd Alexander; ere from Troy
Spread o'er the deep my bark's audacious wings,
To win that face whose glory lights the world.
But she, a nymph nursed in all magic lore
Of herbs and stones, and of the oracular stars,
When, at the mighty summoning of my fate,
I burst from the wild clinging of her arms,
Said only : " When thou liest wounded to death
For Helen's sake, thou wilt come back to me
To give thee life ; till which, my hour, farewell ! "
Then suddenly, fiercely kissed me, and was gone.

HELENA.

And hath she power, think'st thou, to heal this wound ?

PARIS.

No leech but she or Death can give me ease.

HELENA.

Then shall my message drink the winds of speed.

PARIS.

Where dost thou go?   What message wouldst thou
send?

HELENA.

To crave for her false love Œnone's aid.

PARIS.

Rouse not the jealous tempest of her soul!

HELENA.

Let jealous minds be jealous of their peers, .
Not she of Helena!   Let her brew me drink
Of easeful poppies, with Circean spell
To lull me to Elysium—give me death
In that still potion for the feverish blood
That gives thee life: I'll thank her for the boon.

PARIS.

O torturer, earth could live without the sun
Easier than I, thou knowest, without thy face!
Leave me not, Helen, or come quickly back;
For the grudged moments when I see thee not
Will stretch to years of torment, burning here!

Υ.

PARIS, CHORUS.

PARIS.

Alas! this wound. Alas! this festering fire!

Strophe a.

CHORUS.

We wail thy wound, and our country's dole!

PARIS.

Can ye make me whole?

CHORUS.

For thy shafts must slumber, unbent thy bow

PARIS.

As of one laid low!

CHORUS.

We wail for Troy, and the fires of Troy
In thy fate and fires !

PARIS.

Wail for the world, and the end of joy
And the heart's desires !

Strophe β.

CHORUS.

Alas ! of an evil day for the evil hour
When Hermes laid in thy hand our bale in the baleful
    fruit,
And, a mortal judging Immortals, to thee, to the fatal
    bower,
Came flushed the Olympian Three, in divine dispute ;
And Hera stepped on the sward in the sultry, thun-
    derous noon
Of her beauty's opulent pride—sad-eyed as new-
    springing day,
August as night, with the stars in her train, and the
    mighty moon

For brooch on her splendid shoulder—a queen in
    superb array ;

And Pallas, calm in her claim, stood stern ; with no
    wanton's art,

An athlete bared for the strife, disdaining her martial
    vest :

O, then did thy heart not leap to adore her, as leaps
    the heart

At tale of a hero's death, at the gleam of her virgin
    breast !

But last, with her siren smile, the siren child of the sea

Came tripping with foam-like feet o'er the dazzled
    and glowing grass ;

Her charms beamed mistily coy as she luringly smiled
    on thee,

Scarce lifting her roseate veil, and sang in thine ear—
    alas !

PARIS.

Who may divide the evil from the good,
Or in the bud, or in the perfect flower?

Antistrophe a.
CHORUS.

We rue the evil in flower and bud !

Paris.

I, this burning blood !

Chorus.

For thy evil climbs to its flowering day !

Paris.

And my heart grows clay !

Chorus.

We rue the wounds of our falling state
In thy fall and wound !

Paris.

Rue the vain strife of the soul with fate,
And the spheres untuned !

Antistrophe β.

Chorus.

O, better thou hadst not been, or hadst ne'er been
    given
By Ida back to thy sire, our blood on thy golden
    head ;

That, a shepherd piping to Dryads aloft where the
earth meets heaven,

The store of thy quiver had been but the panther's
dread !

The rathe delight of the chase, or the noonday slum-
berous lair

And Œnone's passionate arms, were better for us and
thee ;

The hot grey lavender's breath, and the balm of
thyme in her hair,

Than Helen, and reeking war, for the spoil of the
conquered sea !

And sweeter murmured the winds at eve in the sighing pines

Than ocean's weltering waves afoam at the plunging
prow :

O, hissed not the siren snake of the treacherous
gleaming brine,

Some boding of dreadful death, and the horror that
hems us now !

For then was thy day of choice ; but now the day of
thy doom

O'ertakes thee with thunder-tread, and the sorrows
that we have seen

Are pale regrets that grow dim as we enter the van-
    ward gloom ;
For we are the thralls of thy fate—O, better thou
    hadst not been !

PARIS.

The moment's tongue that sums up weal and woe
Is by its new-born brother's made a liar.

CHORUS.

Alas ! all moments now chime in one tale,
And our last hope comes visaged like despair.

Ⴤ.

ŒNONE, PARIS, CHORUS.

PARIS.

Thou bloodless spectre of a love that once
Honour slew bleeding, from what grave of dreams
Comest thou to haunt me now, and pale, so pale, ·
To scare me with thy melancholy eyes?

ŒNONE.

What from Œnone now craves Helen's lord ? ·

PARIS.

O silver-footed syllables of woe

Thronging the startled porches of mine ear
With delicate invasion ; dovelike tones
Of that forgotten and familiar voice !
Like sad, sweet funeral flutes ye stir my hair,
Sounding within my soul marches of doom.
Comest thou, Œnone, now to look on me ?

ŒNONE.

What wouldst thou with me, Paris ?   I am here.

PARIS.

Death was thy herald.   Nymph, thine hour is come !

ŒNONE.

Else were the gods a lie.   Where is thy wound ?

PARIS.

Here flame the mouths of quenchless Tartarus.

ŒNONE.

Bribe all the summoned surgery of the world
With Priam's treasure, or with Helen's charms,
And bid it cure thee—vain were all its drugs !

PARIS.

I know it ; and therefore have I sent for thee.

ŒNONE.

Ha ! ha ! What salve hast thou to heal my wound ?
What martial vitriol—fire to drive out fire ?
What poppied sleep to soothe an aching heart ?
What sovereign gums—myrrh, or opopanax,
Or pectoral bdellium, or warm zedoary,
To balm this anguish ?   What Lethean wine
Of hemlock wilt thou give my soul to drink,
Taming with poison poison ?   Wilt thou charm
Its mystery from the orient stone, bezoar,
Oozed from the eyes of serpent-eating stags,
To suck from out my breast the venom here
Festering these age-long years—love turned to hate ?

PARIS.

Hate me or love, my life is in thy hand :
Yet to thy love I sue not, nor thy hate ;
Nor shall my soul with forward-gazing eyes
Tread back the devious by-ways of the past.
Meet we nor friends nor foes ; but look on me

As on thy dying king—Troy with my fall
Falling, Troy burning in my burning.   Thou,
Nymph of dark thoughts, to whom the Lord of Light
Hath given to lift the veil of the world, to find
Virtue in things of bale, from deadliest worts
To charm benign drops of balsamic dew;
Thou with grave, healing eyes shouldst front the
　　Fates
Passionless as themselves.   Let not thy will
Be miser of thy power ; but, saving me,
Save not a man once loved, though hated now,
Save Troy, thy country, and live honoured more
Than Hector dead !   Or, if thy humbler needs
Crave lowlier wealth, ask, and be satisfied.

ŒNONE.

My king ! My country ! And she, my gracious queen,
Helen, what will she give me ?   Will she smile,
And let me kiss her condescending hand ?
Go, mend thy wit, or have respect to mine !
Fool ! for what fee should I thy recreant head
Ransom from merited ruin ?   Or shall I trust
Once more the honeyed glozing of thy tongue,
And bargain that from out the quaking courts

Of thy beleaguered soul my sorcery's might
Shall drive Death's ghastly minions, torture and fear ;
That thee, poor trembler o'er the abyss of gloom,
Will I give back to Helen and to life ;
And for this aid beg but some golden urn
To hide love's ashes in—to smile upon,
Or weep upon, mayhap, what is it to thee,
Since I am naught?   What guerdon, ye just gods !
What generous guerdon for my king to pay !

Paris.

Then I must die, and guiltless Troy burn up ;
And stalking through her streets—red shamble-pools
Of fire-reflecting blood—murder gone mad,
With crimson horror blazon silvery heads,
Toss babes for sport to the flames ; young maids
        must shriek,
First orphaned, and then ravished ; matrons feel
The whips of slavery ; that thy rage may gloat
Upon my torment !   Go !   Leave me to Death !

Œnone.

And wherefore not ?   Thy blood on thine own head !

PARIS.

Go then ! Tread back the dim familiar ways
Strange with new whispering horror—go ! Live on !
Read the black tale to the end ! Lone in thy den,
Couched with thy fawning leopards, watch Troy burn,
While thy fierce hands drag down their heavy heads
To warm thy merciless breast. Say to thy soul :
"This is my work !" and be for evermore
The prey of memories dreadful as the shades
Lured by the blood of tombs. For evermore
Thy mountain streams shall taint thy lips like blood,
The heavy-splashing thunder-drops shall seem
Hot blood upon thy brow; for evermore
Thy fancy-sickened ear shall hear all night,
Hissing among the pine-tops murmuring cool,
Thy burning kindred's curses—live accurst !

ŒNONE.

Waste not on me, Paris, thy dying breath :
Go frighten Helen with thy evermores.

PARIS.

They sing but idly in thine ear; for still

All this is but the pattern of thy thought
Woven on the fleeting air : thou art too great
For such a baseness.   Born of Death and Life,
Twinned with her sister Justice Vengeance came,
To walk with her the world ; not in blind rage
Smite, for the shepherd's crime, the innocent fold ;
And thou, being just in hate, wilt, hating me,
Hate more injustice ; thou wilt bid me live,
And Troy defy the jealousy of the gods.

ŒNONE.

It is too late to stay the bolt of doom
Launched by thy hand, and fallen upon thy head.
O traitor ! thou didst kindle in my breast
The flames of Troy ; hast reft me of all power
Of ruth, remorse, or fear ; dungeoned in stone
My human senses, till their ceaseless ache
Throbs through the aching darkness where they sit
Holding no parley with the world of day.
Fool ! when the long hours in procession slow :
The weeping, bleeding hours ; the hours of rage ;
The stony-eyed, dull, apathetic hours ;
The hours that plucked up hope to brew despair,
That tortured love to hate, and made my brain

A cage of madness : when the unhasting march
Of stolid hours, blank to my craving gaze,
Brings now the destined and long-waited one
Which drags thee to my feet, shall I grow mild?
No; let thy soul go sickening down from day,
Burn thou and Troy; love, hate; burn all the world;
Then let me leap to death, beholding doom,
Find in revenge release, and feel no more !

PARIS.

Alas ! that, erring from its wholesome walk,
Thy solitary spirit, dowered to win
From poison healing, in this brooding gloom
Should choose to sit, a sorceress in her cave
Wringing from flowers malignant honey-dew.

ŒNONE.

Hear him, ye gods !   Who made me what I am?
Methinks I teem with all the festering woe
In all the cankered hearts of women true
Begotten by false men ; bring forth on thee
Terrible vengeance for an ancient wrong
Bittering the winds and blighting all the world.

F

PARIS.

O, must I die !   Canst thou endure to look
On torments which my slayer's pitiless eye
Might in self-pity shrink from?   Am I false
To love ; or thou, whose love, in naught but hate
Horribly constant, clings about my heart
Like jealous Deianeira's fiery robe ?

ŒNONE.

What torture scathes like the revenge of love
The avenger with the amerced ?   What are thy pangs
To mine ; thy sufferings to my cursed joy
To see thee suffer ?   Would that thou and I
Lay here dead !   Yet I would not cheat the august
Erinnys of slain love of that brief hour
Wherein we burn upon her holy pyre
Of retribution ; not yet must we die.

PARIS.

Nay ; yet we must not die.   Let saner thoughts
Talk with thy madness.   Who is false to love :
I, who loved once and loving learnt to love ;
Or thou, who loving ill art fallen to hate ?

ŒNONE.

Love is not love that sips and further flies.

PARIS.

Less is love love that tested turns to hate.

ŒNONE.

Talk on : 'tis long since I have heard that voice
With singing suasion drape its lies in truth.

PARIS.

Truth naked from man's tongue in woman's ear
Stings like a lie; but flattering lies are truth.

ŒNONE.

All's one, then, truthful lies or lying truth :
Sing me to death with that voluptuous voice.

PARIS.

Œnone, we were young; and then young love
Sprang in our hearts a flower of tender flame,
Shy firstling of the spring, and hastening forth
To kiss the gracious coming of her feet ;

Now, since our spring's long over, let us keep
The delicate raptures of its crocus-time
Like dew from the eye of noon : in memory's dim
And odorous aisles like odours let them float ;
For thus though dead they live.   But madly strive
To kiss them quick again, Time's blind revenge
On things untimely strikes them dead indeed,
Making delicious memories craving ghosts.

ŒNONE.

There are no seasons in true lovers' vows
Pledged for eternity, and thy fickle breath
Bound with eternal bonds my faithful heart.
O, how thy candour shows thee black !   How truth,
Come in Death's train, in session on thy lip
Proclaims thee false !   Is thy brief spring run by,
Withered in Helen's arms ?   But mine ?   Behold !
Is spring herself less redolent of spring ?
Am I less comely in thy ranging eye
Than she, the old Œnone of thy love ?
Helen, they say, is fair—am not I fair ?
Though pale with gazing in pale sorrow's face,
Not fair as ever ?   Helen keeps her youth,
Being divine—do not I keep my youth,

A nymph, divine as she?   My eyes to-day,
Out-daring eagles', can at fiery noon
Question the sun ; my feet can leap to-day,
Swift as my father's fountains down the rocks,
Outrun the panther.   Winter, when he came
Last to our upland valleys dumb with snow,
Beheld me grapple with a furious wolf
At prowl around my flock, and hurl him sheer,
Howling, from off the crag.   What tenderest leaf
Fades from my Oread youth ?   Look in my face,
And say am I not fair—as ever fair ?

PARIS.

Fairer than ever, with those glorious eyes
Ablaze like moons out of a stormy sky ;
More fair being pale, who wast the fairest nymph
That ever like its visible spirit moved
Bright through the gladed forest.   'Tis the eye
With which I look on thee is changed, not thou.
I age, o'erwintered with the fleeting years,
And being so changed I am no more thy mate.
Yet heal me, Œnone !   Heal me for the sake,
Fairest Œnone ! of that shepherd youth
Who loved thee with the passion of his spring,

Taught thee to love ! O, give me back my life—
Perchance my spring, which seems to breathe from
     thee,
Which seems to whisper in my dying ear
Regrets, desires——! Quick, quick, put forth thy
     power
Before it be too late ! Œnone, O love !
Put forth thy power, and give me back my spring !

ŒNONE.

I am mad, to put frail new-born hopes to nurse
Upon the haggard bosom of despair :
O false Paris ! false love ! `Swear thou art true,
And I'll believe it. But be true to me,
Dreaming vain dreams no more in Helen's world,
Drugged by the wild nepenthe of her charms,
And glut thy heart with life ! Can Helen love ?
O, let me flood thy being with such love
As Nilus, leaping from his dungeon snow,
On mummied Egypt sheds, and bids her live !
Dead though thou art, my love can raise thee up ;
Enslaved thy soul, I'll set it free again ;
Withered thy spring, I'll pour the bliss of youth
Through all thy parchèd veins. But swear to me,

When all my pride is melted into love,
And all my love in one tumultuous wave
Of healing hath uplifted thee from death,
The Spartan shall not have thee—swear to me !

PARIS.

Bind me not with vain oaths but potent love ;
And if thou hast the love, put forth the power.

ŒNONE.

The power lies in my lips ; but O, beware !
If thou art parleying with a double thought ;
If thou but lovest thy life for Helen's sake ;
If her imperious vision comes to dash
The mystery of our lips, then thou art lost,
And all my power to save thee vainly spilt.

PARIS.

Quick, let me make the ordeal of thy lips !
Sorceress ! I am twice Death's fool ! Come, Helen,
    come !

ŒNONE.

False, false, utterly false ! utterly lost !

Alas ! poor trickster of thyself, I have steeped
My soul in baser elements, have given
My holiest fountains to thy scorching thirst,
My stateliest branches to thy rending—all
Because I loved as never woman man ;
All, knowing thy false heart—in vain ! in vain !
Back to thy Helen—let her save thee now !

PARIS.

Away, thy love is but a clinging curse !
Leave me in peace to die.   My moments run
Like priceless drops of life-blood, and are lost
In thirsty sands ; for Helen is not here.
Come, Helen, Helen, Helen, come to me !

ŒNONE.

Fool ! she is cold as ice—she loves thee not.

PARIS.

What's that to me, who love her, cold as warm ?

ŒNONE.

What, is this naught, loving to be beloved !

PARIS.

Man's soul yearns to be loved, but more to love.

ŒNONE.

What force hath ice to kindle such a fire?

PARIS.

Fate makes all women fond, one beautiful.

ŒNONE.

Thou art besotted of a siren dream,
Whose end is wreck.   Hate's self must pity thee.

PARIS.

Away, and let me dream on her who made
Life an Olympian song!   Thou art a child
With thy weak blustering love, that can but scream
And make no music.   I could chide thee now
As vexed Apollo some monotonist
That will but finger in one mode alone,
And learn no other.   But my sandy drops
With each one thirst burn—O, reprieve me, Death!
Come to me, Helen!   Vanish thou—she comes!

HELENA, ŒNONE, PARIS, CHORUS.

HELENA.

What cry, with dreadful iterance of my name,
Haggards the dying day?   Paris!   O, speak!

ŒNONE.

Now must I die; for I have seen my bane.
Farewell, Paris!   Now, Helen, guard thy theft,
A mightier thief is here—Death, Death, hail Death!

HELENA, PARIS, CHORUS.

CHORUS.

O mighty love, self-slain in slaying her!
O furious passion strangled suddenly!
For dead she is, having with piteous shriek
O'erleaped the battlement, and crushed and dead
Lies; her wild soul shrill in the shrieking air.

PARIS.

Sternly, Œnone, hast thou knelled me hence.
I must die, Helen!   Helen, I must die!

HELENA

Was this, then, flint in bounteous woman's form?

Paris.

All's lost—no more of her ! But let me make
Each quivering pulse-beat of this agony
More rich with love than honey-drops with sweet,
Eternal more than marble monuments
Of heroes dead. Words, words—but kiss me, Helen !

Priam, Hecuba, Helena, Paris, Chorus.

Paris.

O Dis ! my parents claim me, welcome now
As summoning Charon ! Love must harass love—
These aged creatures with their bootless tears
Weep me from Helen ! How now, mother? Ay,
Thy brand is more than kindled—it burns out.

Hecuba.

O luckless day, of many a luckless day
The last and direst ! I have lived too long.

Paris.

Nay, mother, dying now, I have lived too long.

Hecuba.

'Twas but to-day I heard Cassandra shriek,

After long silence—not for naught.   Ye gods
Who hate our stock, where are your thunderbolts?
Strike; make a sudden end; let Troy crash down
On our white heads : but no more deaths of sons!

PRIAM.

O Paris, Paris ! smile this trouble by ;
Bid me take courage with thy wonted look !
Alas ! thou dost undo me with those eyes
Which dully glass the filmèd eyes of Death !

PARIS.

I am wing-stricken, father, and brought down
Upon my upward gyre.   O Troy!   I thought—
No matter—all's too late—I am ebbed too far.

PRIAM.

O Death, couldst thou be cozened, to accept
My palsy for his vigour, to yield up
This royal bud for majesty o'erblown,
How merrily would I dance thy way with thee
When thou didst pluck my beard !   My son ! my son !

PARIS.

Peace, father, lest the passion of thy love

Make me die weeping. Mother, grant me grace,
Even as to one condemned, and come to die;
And now, though in thy breasts the mother's milk,
Soured by the curdling visage of thy dream,
Let starve my lips, ere for thy cherishing care
My want could urge more reason than a wail;
Though from my foundling youth thy kindly love
Throbbed in a fickle fever, warm and cold,
O mother, kiss me once before I die!

HECUBA.

O bitter words, yet just! O ill-starred son,
My fierce and wretched heart knows thee too late;
Forgive thy froward mother—O, forgive!

PARIS.

Nay, thou august of days! twixt thee and me,
Where all is love, forgiveness hath no place.
But now, throng not about me, give me room
To feel the vast serenity of death
Extinguish agony. Farewell, and mourn not!

HECUBA.

What, in our strangered hearts' first greeting hour,
Wilt thou so thrust me forth? Too cruel son,

Let me die here, a dog upon thy grave.

PARIS.

Nay, be more kind : thy poignancy of grief
But lends new sharpness to the pangs I feel.

PRIAM.

Come, Hecuba ; this semblance of neglect
Is love's best courtesy.   With bleeding hearts
We leave thee at a wish, whom to attend
To life's dark bourne were sorrow's utmost joy.

HECUBA.

Then lead me to my grave : let all farewells
Be swallowed up in one, the last—to life.

HELENA, PARIS, CHORUS.

PARIS.

I must die, Helen ! Helen, I must die—
Must shiver out upon the lonely night
From this warm world of love, my deeds undone,
Go crownless to the shades.   Ah ! pity me !
Thou who alone hast known me, pity me !

HELENA.

Piteous, yet not, in sordid hopes and fears,
Of mortal lots the worst, the life of him
Who strives, and waits his day of strife supreme ;
Who gathers wisdom for the mightier strife
Among his broken weapons ; tames his soul
To learn its valour's range, then with each power
Poised and keen shining like Athena's spear,
To assault the golden portals of success,
Finds but Death waiting there, with bitter waste
To snatch him from the needy world unknown.
Alas ! what cruel comfort lives in words ;
And thou liest there, and I have nought but words !

PARIS.

Dost thou weep, Helen ?   Thy rare-flowing tears
Are comforting elixirs to my soul.
But who shall comfort Troy ?   What dost thou, Death,
Harrying for naught this miserable hive ?
The patient honey of a thousand hours
Spilt in an instant—deeds and the food of deeds
Wasted, and wrecked the home of old renown !

HELENA.

Deeds are but graves and sculptured monuments
Of mightier thoughts, which are the potent winds
Quickening the world's great soul.   I weep for thee,
And ruined Troy, and all the world in thee,
But weeping crown thee ; and my tears, like dew,
Shall keep thy budded laurels green in fame.

PARIS.

Cold cling the leaves of fame round dying brows ;
And I am sinking with yon sinking sun,
On whom I look my last.   How cold he grows !
And my fierce fires burn cold !   Grow not thou cold,
Helen : thou art my sun, shine on me still,
Thy face is all my life !   But thou art pale,
So pale thy dreadful beauty looks like death.

HELENA.

My lips are, as the lips of pity, pale,
Taking thy passion's colour in this kiss.

PARIS.

The drowsy spirit of invincible sleep

Sits heavily on my lids, and on my feet
Death binds his leaden sandals.   I must sleep—
To wake, ah! where?   Where Helen will not be!

HELENA.

I know not; for some elemental change
Is whispering in my blood.   Come hence with me!

PARIS.

Ay, help me hence.   Upon that golden bed,
The world's true centre, where, with dreadful orbs
Propitiously conjunct, the star of love
Reigned in my house of life, there will I die.
Sing me to sleep; and let but Helen's voice
Mate me in dreams with Helen, I die great.
Flatter me once—I have not fooled myself—
I ravished thee from Sparta all too weak
To storm with love thy heart's impregnable
Virginity; yet, dying, let me sink
Into a passionate dream, the best and last.
Come, Helen, in that dream; stoop to me once;
Ravish my soul forth in one burning kiss,
And all this fiery torment shall seem love!

Chorus.

Strophe α.

O, dire the ruin, dark the day,
When on the path of a rushing woe
Pale troops of tardy-gaited prayers
Halt vainly, loud too late
With unavailing wailing!

Antistrophe α.

O life of mortals, linked by law
Darkly to powers that we darkly dread
Not know, nor know why man's desire
Should bring forth joy to-day,
But on the morrow, sorrow!

Strophe β.

Wherefore, alas! should we call any more
On the name of any god?
For they desert us who should befriend us,
And swift are the bolts of their wrath to rend us,
Slow their pity to heal our sore!

Antistrophe β.

Tangled is man from his birth in a maze
And the toughening coils of fate!

Desires, like babes, to their hunger bind him,
And Ignorance hoar, with her torch, behind him
Lights the error of trackless ways !

Κ

HELENA, CHORUS.

HELENA.

Split is the veteran oak ; untimely lopt
From Priam's trunk the last heroic bough :
Paris is dead ; and sudden-blazing Troy
Shall be his funeral pyre.   Now comes the night
Wherein I vanish from the wondering world ;
But on the ever-opening scroll of Time
Must Helen's name, in fiery characters,
Flourish in dreadful blazon.   Lying Fame,
Hissing, with all her tongues at brazen war,
Will slander me with base detracting spite.
And baser praise ; but, like the moon serene
Above the raging billows, I shall smile.
Lightnings of heaven, and you, ye eternal stars,
Spirits of elemental air and fire
Which keep your courses silently as the Fates,
Ye winds of morn, and ethers of dim day,
Assume me to yourselves, with you to reign !

CHORUS.

Evil and good the august Uranian Fates
Brought blind into the world, protæan twins
Of double mind, each with the other's face,
To rule, for hidden ends, the life of man :
But them he rules who smites with dauntless hand
The lyre of life, chanting some Orphic song.

THE END.

PRINTED BY WILLIAM CLOWES AND SONS, LIMITED,
LONDON AND BECCLES.

www.ingramcontent.com/pod-product-compliance
Lightning Source LLC
Chambersburg PA
CBHW020042030726
47499CB00007B/2537